# Pakkun the Wolf and His Dinosaur Friends

**Written and Illustrated by Yasuko Kimura**

One of Mrs. Hen's eggs rolls out of her nest.

Oh no! The egg has fallen down a hole. It has disappeared.
"I'll find it for you," said Pakkun the Wolf.
"Please be careful, Pakkun!" cried Mrs. Hen.

"Where am I?" Pakkun asked.
"What a strange place this is!"
"Ha, ha, ha!" a little voice laughed,
"Welcome to the Land of Dinosaurs!"

"Excuse me," said Pakkun. "My name is Pakkun.
I am looking for Mrs. Hen's egg.
Have you seen it anywhere?"
"No, I haven't." said the very strange creature.
"Maybe it fell into the sea."

"Pakkun, I want to help you
find Mrs. Hen's egg,"
said the little creature.

"My name is Pteranodon, but you can call me Ptera.
Let's be friends."
"Okay, let's search in the sea!" Pakkun exclaimed.
Glub, glub, glub. Pakkun and Ptera swim into the sea.
But they do not find Mrs. Hen's egg.

"Let's climb onto my mother's back and
look from the sky," suggested Ptera.
Pakkun and Ptera look everywhere.
But they still do not see Mrs. Hen's egg.

"I've had enough. I want to get down!" cried Pakkun. "Please let me down!"

"Pardon me, Mr. T-Rex," said Ptera.
"Have you seen Mrs. Hen's egg?"
"Sorry, but we haven't seen any eggs,"
replied Mr. T-Rex.

"Grrrr! You look tasty!" roared a huge creature.
"Oh no! It's Karaurus," yelled Ptera,
"and he's always hungry!"

"I'm scared, Pakkun!" said Ptera, trembling. "Grrrr," Pakkun the Wolf bares his fangs at Karaurus, and scares him away.

"An egg, you say?" Mrs. Saurapod asked.
"Why don't you try the Valley of Dinosaur
Eggs near Mount Sulphur.
You might find it there."

The road to Mount Sulphur is long and hot.
"I can't take another step!" cried Pakkun.
"You can do it!" urged Ptera.
"We're almost there."

If they just climb down here…

"We made it!"
they both cheered.
"Wow, there are
so many eggs!"

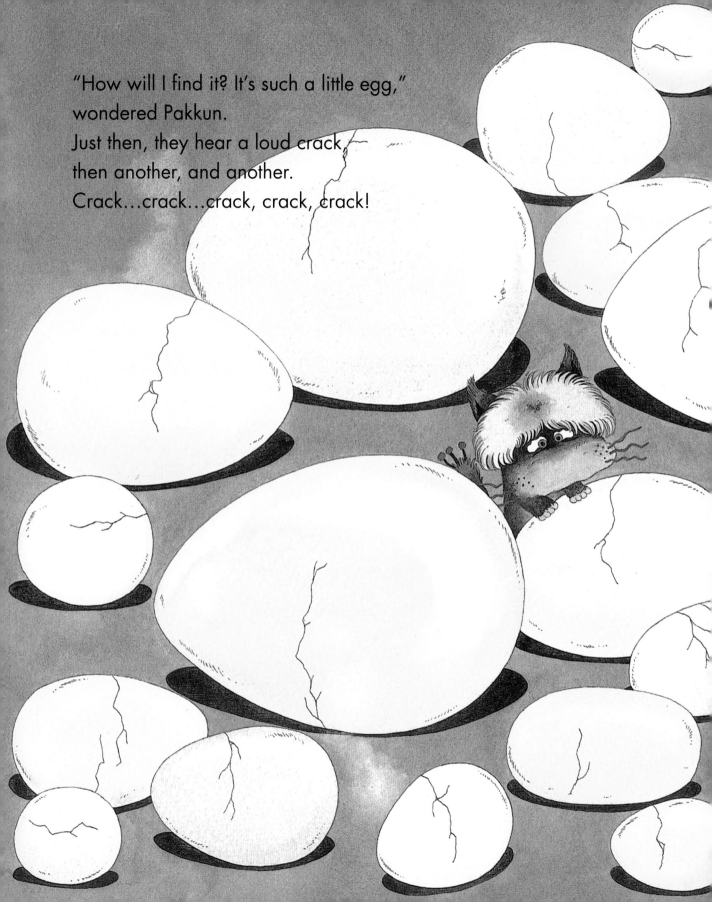

"How will I find it? It's such a little egg,"
wondered Pakkun.
Just then, they hear a loud crack,
then another, and another.
Crack...crack...crack, crack, crack!

Wow! What a sight! All of the eggs have hatched at the same time!

"Look, I've found Mrs. Hen's egg!"
Ptera exclaimed.
"It is the smallest egg."
"That's it! That's it! A baby chick has
hatched from it," said Pakkun.

"I must take the chick back to
Mrs. Hen," said Pakkun.
"Well, goodbye my new friend,"
said Ptera. "Take care!"
"Thank you, Ptera," said Pakkun,
"I'll never forget you!"

"How wonderful!" exclaimed Mrs. Hen,
beaming with joy.
"All of the other eggs have hatched, too.
Thank you, Pakkun the Wolf!"

That night, Pakkun the Wolf dreams that Ptera
and all his other dinosaur friends come out to
play with him.

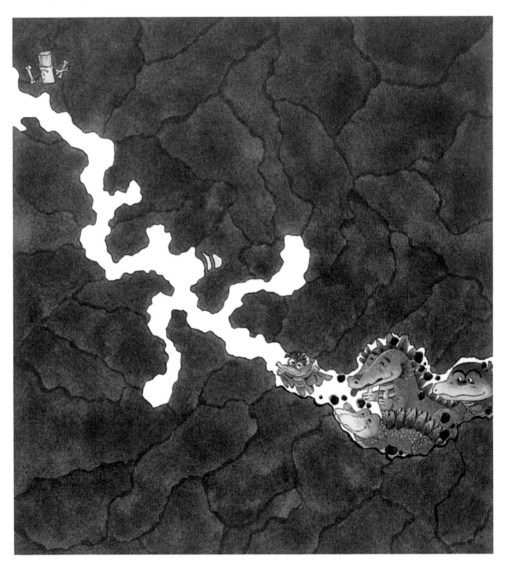

**PAKKUN THE WOLF AND HIS DINOSAUR FRIENDS**

Pakkun Okami to Kyouryu tachi © 1982 Yasuko Kimura
All rights reserved.

Translation by Aoi Taniguchi Roberts
English editing by Richard Stull

ISBN 978-1-940842-04-2
Printed in Shenzhen, Guangdong, China     0150501

Published in the United States by:

MUSEYON INC.
1177 Avenue of the Americas, 5th Floor
New York, NY 10036

Museyon is a registered trademark.
Visit us online at www.museyon.com

Originally published in Japan in 1982 by POPLAR Publishing Co., Ltd.
English translation rights arranged with POPLAR Publishing Co., Ltd.